You Are
Special

A Story for Everyone

ILLUSTRATIONS BY SERGIO MARTINEZ

Max Lucado

CROSSWAY BOOKS · WHEATON, ILLINOIS

PUBLISHER'S ACKNOWLEDGMENT

The publisher wishes to acknowledge that the text for *You Are Special* appeared originally in *Tell Me the Secrets*, written by Max Lucado and illustrated by Ron DiCianni.

You Are Special
Text copyright ©1993, 1997, 2002 by Max Lucado
Illustrations ©1997, 2002 by Sergio Martinez
Published by Crossway Books *a division of Good News Publishers*
1300 Crescent Street, Wheaton, Illinois 60187

Design by UDG | DesignWorks, Sisters, Oregon
First printing 2002
Printed in the United States of America and bound in Mexico

LIBRARY OF CONGRESS CATALOGING-IN-PUBLICATION DATA

Lucado, Max.
You are special : a story for everyone / Max Lucado ; illustrations by
Sergio Martinez. — [Special gift ed. for adults]
  p. cm.
ISBN 1-58134-405-8 (hc : alk. paper)
1. Self-esteem--Fiction. 2. Toys--Fiction. I. Martinez, Sergio, 1937-ill. II. Title.
PS3562.U225 Y68 2002
813'.54--dc21

                              2001007946

11   10   09   08   07   06   05   04   03   02
15 14 13 12 11 10 9 8 7 6 5 4 3 2 1

To the Parents of the Children
at Oak Hills Church

THE
WEMMICKS

THE WEMMICKS were small wooden people carved by a woodworker named Eli. His workshop sat on a hill overlooking their village.

Each Wemmick was different. Some had big noses, others had large eyes. Some were tall and others were short. Some wore hats, others wore coats. But all were made by the same carver, and all lived in the village.

And all day, every day, the Wemmicks did the same thing: They gave each other stickers. Each Wemmick had a box of golden star stickers and a box of gray dot stickers. Up and down the streets all over the city, people spent their days sticking stars or dots on one another.

The pretty ones, those with smooth wood and fine paint, always got stars. But if the wood was rough or the paint chipped, the Wemmicks gave dots.

The talented ones got stars, too. Some could lift big sticks high above their heads or jump over tall boxes. Still others knew big words or could sing pretty songs. Everyone gave them stars.

Some Wemmicks had stars all over them! Every time they got a star, it made them feel so good! It made them want to do something else and get another star.

Others, though, could do little. They got dots.

Punchinello was one of these. He tried to jump high like the others, but he always fell. And when he fell, the others would gather around and give him dots.

Sometimes when he fell, his wood got scratched, so the people would give him more dots.

Then when he would try to explain why he fell, he would say something silly, and the Wemmicks would give him more dots.

After a while he had so many dots that he didn't want to go outside. He was afraid he would do something dumb such as forget his hat or step in the water, and then people would give him another dot. In fact, he had so many gray dots that some people would come up and give him one for no reason at all.

"He deserves lots of dots," the wood-en people would agree with one another.

"He's not a good wooden person."

After a while Punchinello believed them. "I'm not a good Wemmick," he would say.

The few times he went outside, he hung around other Wemmicks who had a lot of dots. He felt better around them.

LUCIA

ONE DAY Punchinello met a Wemmick who was unlike any he'd ever met. She had no dots or stars. She was just wooden. Her name was Lucia.

It wasn't that people didn't try to give her stickers; it's just that the stickers didn't stick. Some of the Wemmicks admired Lucia for having no dots, so they would run up and give her a star. But it would fall off.

Others would look down on her for having no stars, so they would give her a dot. But it wouldn't stay either.

That's the way I want to be, thought Punchinello.

I don't want anyone's marks.

So he asked the stickerless Wemmick how she did it.

"It's easy," Lucia replied. "Every day I go see Eli."

"Eli?"

"Yes, Eli. The woodcarver. I sit in the workshop with him."

"Why?"

"Why don't you find out for yourself? Go up the hill. He's there." And with that the Wemmick who had no stickers turned and skipped away.

"But will he want to see me?" Punchinello cried out. Lucia didn't hear.

So Punchinello went home. He sat near a window and watched the wooden people as they scurried around giving each other stars and dots.

"It's not right," he muttered to himself. And he decided to go see Eli.

THE
WOODCARVER

PUNCHINELLO walked up the narrow path to the top of the hill and stepped into the big shop. His wooden eyes widened at the size of everything. The stool was as tall as he was. He had to stretch on his tiptoes to see the top of the workbench. A hammer was as long as his arm. Punchinello swallowed hard. "I'm not staying here!" And he turned to leave.

Then he heard his name.

"Punchinello?" The voice was deep and strong.

Punchinello stopped.

"Punchinello! How good to see you. Come and let me have a look at you."

Punchinello turned slowly and looked at the large bearded craftsman. "You know my name?" the little Wemmick asked.

"Of course I do. I made you."

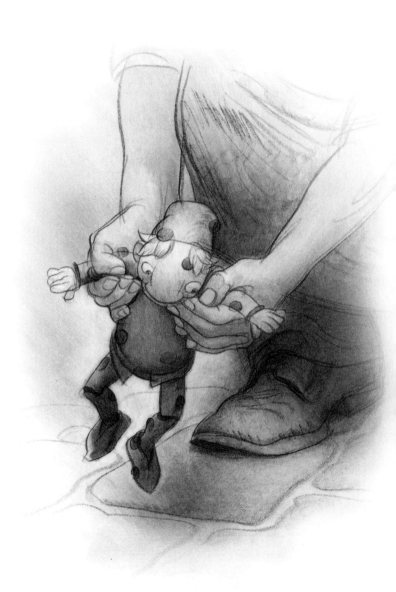

Eli stooped down and picked him up and set him on the bench. "Hmm," the maker spoke thoughtfully as he looked at the gray dots. "Looks like you've been given some bad marks."

"I didn't mean to, Eli. I really tried hard."

"Oh, you don't have to defend yourself to me, child."

"I don't care what the other Wemmicks think."

"You don't?"

"No, and you shouldn't either. Who are they to give stars or dots? They're Wemmicks just like you. What they think doesn't matter, Punchinello. All that matters is what I think. And I think you are pretty special."

Punchinello laughed. "Me, special? Why? I can't walk fast. I can't jump. My paint is peeling. Why do I matter to you?"

Eli looked at Punchinello, put his hands on those small wooden shoulders, and spoke very slowly. "Because you're mine. That's why you matter to me."

Punchinello had never had anyone look at him like this—much less his maker. He didn't know what to say.

"Every day I've been hoping you'd come," Eli explained.

"I came because I met someone who had no marks," said Punchinello.

"I know. She told me about you."

"Why don't the stickers stay on her?"

The maker spoke softly. "Because she has decided that what I think is more important than what they think. The stickers only stick if you let them."

"What?"

"The stickers only stick if they matter to you. The more you trust my love, the less you care about their stickers."

"I'm not sure I understand."

Eli smiled. "You will, but it will take time. You've got a lot of marks. For now, just come to see me every day and let me remind you how much I care."

Eli lifted Punchinello off the bench and set him on the floor.

"Remember," Eli said as the Wemmick walked out the door, "you are special because I made you. And I don't make mistakes."

Punchinello didn't stop, but in his heart he thought, *I think he really means it.*

And when he did, a dot fell to the ground.